HEROES

Written by **KEN MOCHIZUKI**

Illustrated by **DOM LEE**

LEE & LOW BOOKS Inc. • *New York*

*To the men and women of Asian and
Pacific Islander descent who served in the
U.S. armed forces and defended America
with little or no recognition.*—K.M.

To my mom and dad.—D.L.

The insignia that accompanies the Author's Note is a replica of
that of the 442nd Regimental Combat Team. This same insignia
inspired the border for the cover type.

Text copyright © 1995 by Ken Mochizuki
Illustrations copyright © 1995 by Dom Lee
All rights reserved. No part of the contents of this
book may be reproduced by any means without
the written permission of the publisher.
LEE & LOW BOOKS, Inc., 228 East 45th Street, New York, NY 10017
Printed in Hong Kong by South China Printing Co. (1988) Ltd.
Book Design by Christy Hale
Book Production by Our House
The text is set in Trump Medieval
The illustrations are rendered by applying encaustic beeswax on paper,
then scratching out images, and finally adding oil paint for color.

10   9   8   7   6   5   4   3   2   1
First Edition

Library of Congress Cataloging-in-Publication Data
Mochizuki, Ken
Heroes/by Ken Mochizuki; illustrated by Dom Lee. — 1st ed.
p.   cm.
Summary: Japanese American Donnie, whose playmates insist he be
the "bad guy" in their war games, calls on his reluctant father and
uncle to help him get away from that role.
ISBN 1-880000-16-4 (hardcover)
[1. Japanese Americans—Fiction.] I. Lee, Dom, ill. II. Title.
PZ7.M71284He 1995
[Fic]—dc20   94-26541
CIP   AC

AUTHOR'S NOTE

About 50,000 Americans of Asian and Pacific Islander descent served in the armed forces of the United States during World War II. Among the most notable was the 442nd Regimental Combat Team, an all-Japanese American Army regiment that fought in Europe and became one of the most highly decorated units in U.S. Army history.

My dad drove me to school every morning, but I wished he wouldn't. That was because other kids walking to school always turned around and stared. Some pointed, and others pretended their fingers were guns and aimed at us.

"How come we're always the bad guys?" I asked my dad.

"That's only in the movies," he replied.

Still, if I could talk my dad into it, I had him pull the truck over and drop me off down the street from school.

After school, I got together with my friends. I tried to start a football game, but they wanted to play war. Again. That was because they had an enemy to fight: Me. Tori had all the toy guns, and Zach and Reggie always helped bring them to the woods at the end of the street where I met them.

Zach usually brought something that was his dad's. He showed us pictures of his father in the war or some of his medals. "He was a war hero," Zach said, and then repeated how I always had to be the enemy when we played war because I looked like them.

"Get moving, Donnie," Zach commanded. "You're the bad guy, and we're going to hunt you down."

"No, I'm not," I protested. "My dad was in our army and he fought in Italy and France. And my Uncle Yosh was in Korea."

"No way!" Zach said.

"How could your dad or uncle be in *our* army?" Tori asked.

"Yeah," Reggie agreed, "there wasn't anybody looking like you guys on our side. If you can't prove it, you better start hiding, Donnie."

I couldn't prove it, so I had to be the bad guy again. I hated it. Still, it was better than having no friends at all.

But I knew my dad had stories that could prove he was a hero. I sometimes overheard him talking with his army buddies at the gas station. I probably asked him a hundred times to tell me the old war stories, but each time he just shook his head.

Once, I tried to unpin the war medals from my dad's veteran's cap at home to show everybody. I got into trouble for doing that. When I told him that I needed something to prove he was a war hero, he just said, "You kids should be playing something else besides war."

Uncle Yosh was the same way. He sat in the station with us, drinking his coffee, but he was always quiet and never talked about Korea. One time, I asked him about it.

"Real heroes don't brag," he said. "They just do what they are supposed to do."

When he came to our house, he didn't like me watching war shows on TV, or even news about a new war in a country called Vietnam.

I hated being the enemy so much that I decided to hide so my friends would never find me. I stepped quietly through the woods. Beams of sunlight shone between the trees. I kept going into the forest, farther than I ever had before. The sun faded away and the woods got darker. All I heard was my shoes crunching twigs.

Then something rustled in the bushes. It wasn't Tori, Zach, or Reggie.

I was scared. I knew I had to find my way out of there. But what if I had been walking around in circles? I sat down on a big rock and tried to think, because the worst thing I could do was panic. Heroes don't panic. They just do what they are supposed to do.

As Captain Donnie Okada, I led my men slowly, surely, and calmly through the thick forest until I saw sunlight in the distance. I came out into a clearing; it was good to feel the sun again.

"Pow!"

"We got you now, Donnie!"

Zach and Reggie ran toward me in the clearing. I dropped my toy gun and dashed through the woods. Heading down a trail, I tripped and slid most of the way on the seat of my pants, then ran as fast as I could.

Those guys chased me all the way to my dad's gas station—they wouldn't quit.

"Rat-tat-tat-tat! Pow! Pow! Pow! You're dead, Donnie!"

Uncle Yosh hurried out from underneath a car he and Dad were fixing. Uncle Yosh looked mad. Dad got up, too, to see what was going on.

"I'm not the bad guy!" I cried, running to my dad's place. Dad put his hand on my shoulder.

"Come on, kids," he said. "Donnie has had enough."

Uncle Yosh stared at the toy guns and looked even madder.

"Aw, Donnie, you're no fun!" Reggie said.

I looked up at my dad. I almost yanked the pockets off his oily gas station coveralls when I pleaded with him.

"See, Dad, can't you tell me anything? Can't you let me prove it to them? Can't we be heroes, too?"

My dad looked at Uncle Yosh. Uncle Yosh took a moment to think, then he nodded in agreement.

"We'll pick you up at school tomorrow," my dad said.

At school the next day, the kids called me "sissy" and "daddy's boy." Finally, the bell rang and I headed toward the door. My classmates walked together in a big group and followed me. "Hey, Donnie!" someone called out. Then they all pointed at me with their fingers like guns.

"Rat-tat-tat-tat! Pow! Pow!"

They chased me down the hallway. I hoped Dad and Uncle Yosh showed up like they said they would.

Outside, all the kids were excited and pointed to something down the street. I looked that way and couldn't believe my eyes.

My dad stood by his truck with his coveralls on. But he was also wearing sunglasses and his veteran's cap with medals all over it—more than I had seen before. And I couldn't believe Uncle Yosh. He also wore sunglasses along with his uniform and officer's hat. All the ribbons on his chest looked like the top of an open crayon box. His decorations and shiny brass buttons gleamed in the sun.

Uncle Yosh held my football in his hand, and when he found me in the crowd, he shouted, "Hey, Donnie, catch!" He threw a perfect spiral.

Instead of driving me home like I thought was the plan, my dad and Uncle Yosh stuck around for a little while to make sure I would be okay. Then they drove off, leaving me there holding the football.

"Who wants to play?" I asked.

Zach, Reggie, Tori and a bunch of other kids did, so we ran off to the playground.

This time, they were following me instead of chasing me.